Underpants thunderpants!

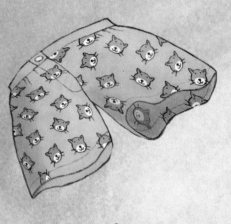

First published in Great Britain in 2011 by Parragon

ISBN 978-0-545-55296-7

12 11 10 9 8 7 6 5   13 14 15 16 17 18/0

Printed in the U.S.A.

First Scholastic printing, March 2013

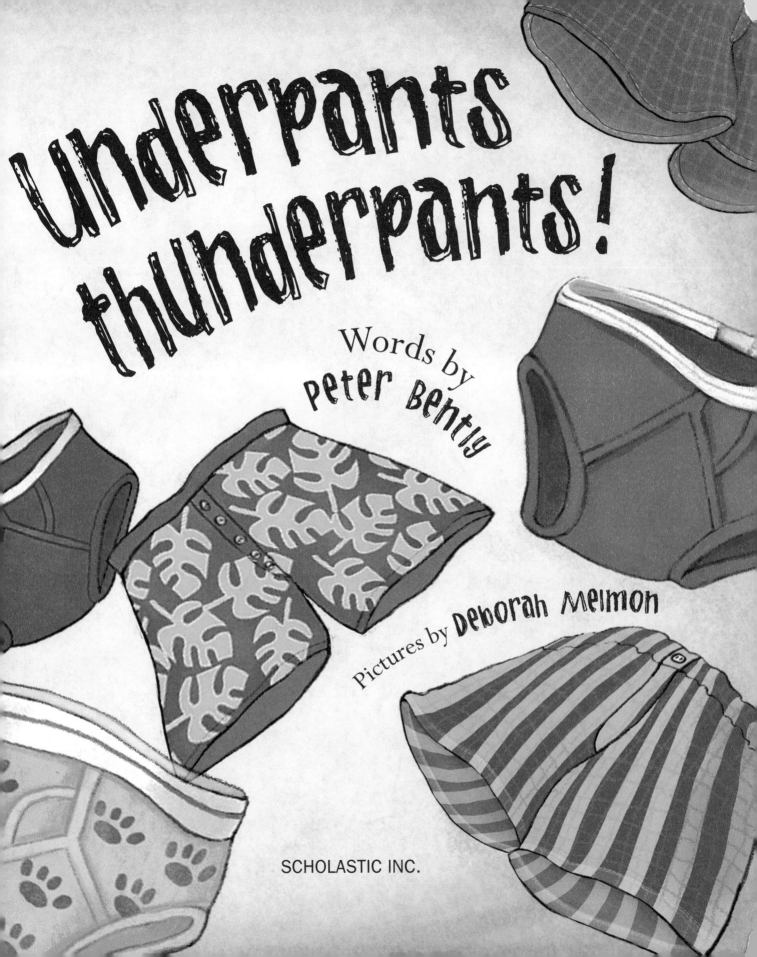

underpants thunderpants!

Words by
peter Bently

Pictures by Deborah Melmon

SCHOLASTIC INC.

One day
when the weather is
sunny and **fine**,
DOG hangs his
underpants
out on the line.

But **thunder** and **lightning** soon fill up the sky.

underpants
thunderpants!

Look at them
fly!

Over the **OCEAN**, the **JUNGLE**, and **TOWN**— where will those **UNDIES** come **fluttering** down?

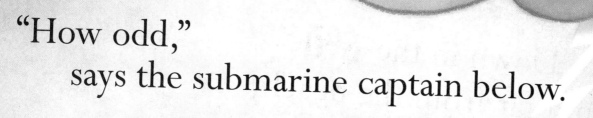

"How odd,"
    says the submarine captain below.

"First I saw **lightning**
        and now I see **snow!**"

Down in the **sea**
not far from the beach,
"A giant!
A giant!"
the little fish
screech.

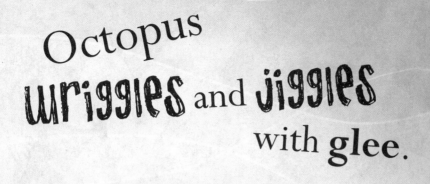

Octopus **wriggles** and **jiggles** with **glee**.

"**Four** pairs of **underpants** perfect for me!"

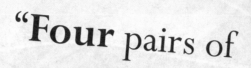

underpants plunderpants!

Just imagine that!

Roger the Pirate
has got a
new **hat!**

Safe out of sight of the **croc's** hungry eyes,

Monkey's discovered a **cunning** disguise!

Elephant's **trunk** has been **tickled** by bees. **"Oh bother,"** he grumbles. "I'm going to **sneeze**, but I don't have a tissue. **What** shall I do?"

"A jumbo-sized hankie! How handy!— ATCHOO!"

Watch it!
A hunter is
down with a
thud.
underpants
blunderpants!
Splat in the **mud!**

Up at the **palace,** the **King** says,
"**Oh my!**
Three pairs of **underpants** baked in a pie!"

A **two-headed** alien

stares from

his **lair**...

"Underpants
wonderpants!
Now I'm
not **bare!**"

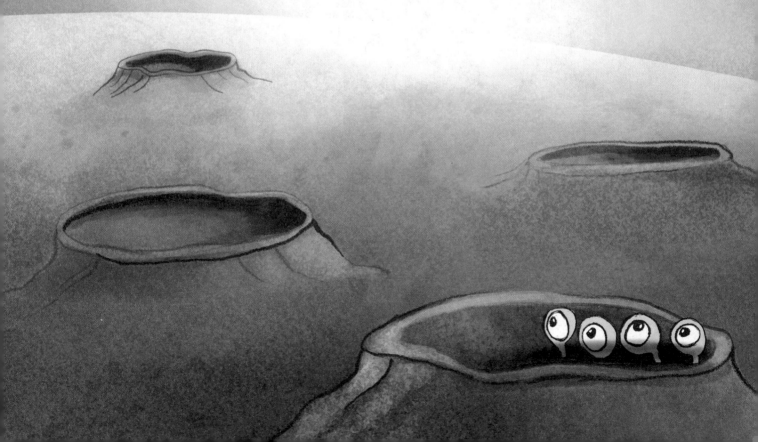